The Road 1

Published by Writers Block Publishing LLC

www.writersblockpublishingllc

Written by E. Davis

www.edavisllc.com

1

JOYCE TIES THE APRON around her waist as she watches Harlem walks across the parking lot enter the coffee shop, Café Moon. Joyce arrived earlier than usual to open the shop. She doesn't want Harlem to want or worry about anything. Joyce made sure the coffees, regular, decaf, and the flavored were beyond fresh-if there is such a thing as beyond fresh coffee. Joyce made sure the pastries, the cookies, donuts, and scones were extra fresh- if there is such a thing as extra fresh pastries. Joyce steps back and admires the scenery. The sun's beams shine through the window. The sun rays hit the tables, making the mahogany tables sparkles; as if there are diamonds dust on the wood. Café Moon is a beautiful coffee shop. The neo-soul style has that cool and relaxed atmosphere. Soul and jazz music plays in the background. There are some booths and tables, tables set for two or four. Joyce is proud of her daughter, Harlem. She is proud of the way Harlem is not allowing anything to distract her from her goals.

"Morning, Mommy," Harlem says, entering Café Moon.

"Morning, baby," Joyce says, smiling. "Look, Harlem, I got everything set real nice."

Harlem eyes scan the coffee shop with a smile.

"Looks good, Mommy." She says, smiling. "Thank you."

"Mark and Candice, they'll be in at seven," Joyce reports.

Harlem looks at the clock; it reads 6:30 A.M.

"Okay, Mommy," Harlem replies. "I'm going to do some paperwork."

Harlem walks to her office.

"Want me to bring you a latte, peppermint, extra expresso?" Joyce offers, smiling.

"Sure, Mommy, thank you," Harlem says.

Harlem enters her office. She turns the light on, the neat, organized, cute, white, and gray office. Pictures of her family and friends are mounted on the wall. Pictures of herself with Stephen, her mother, her brother Steaks, and her father, Big Moon. Harlem sits down at her desk, turns the laptop on, and opens the files to start her day.

Joyce enters the office with Harlem's coffee. She sets the pretty purple coffee cup on the desk with a napkin under the cup. Joyce steps back to admire her tending.

"Thanks, Mommy," Harlem says, not taking her eyes off the computer.

Joyce waits to be dismissed. She waits for Harlem to tell her that she is alright, that she doesn't need anything. Harlem looks at Joyce. Joyce smiles at her daughter.

"I'm good, Mommy," Harlem says.

Joyce nods her head.

"Okay," Joyce says. "I'll be out front."

Joyce turns and walks out of the office. Harlem takes in a deep breath and decides to look at her cell phone. She hopes there is another text message or missed call from Stephen. She looks; there isn't. Just the last text message from Stephen replying back with: "OK."

Just ok.

They reached a dead end. They have come to the point in their relationship that is at the end of the road. One will go left, and the other will go right, but they will not go together. Life has consumed their hope, forcing them to cohabitate just for the sake of; neither of them wanted to be the first to say;

"This is the end."

They haven't attended family functions together anymore. Neither attends important ceremonies. There has been no conversation unless it was about the bills.

"I paid the mortgage," one would say.

"Okay," the other reply. "I'll take care of the car note and insurance."

They went from no lovemaking to sleeping in with their backs to each other to now sleep in separate rooms. Harlem couldn't put her finger on what happened;

"We stopped," she tried explaining to Joyce.

"Stopped what?" Joyce asked.

"Stopped everything," Harlem said. "Then again, I don't think it even began."

HARLEM LOOKS AT THE picture of Big Moon and her on her desk. Big Moon is her father. His name is Walter. Harlem nicknamed him Big Moon because of his size. Big Moon stood tall at six feet, five inches; he had a round, large full moon shape. Big Moon was always a hands-on father. He was loving, patient, yet a strict disciplinarian. He was her full moon. Harlem was daddy's Girl. Whenever she smiled at Big Moon, his heart melted, and he became putty in her hands. Harlem has an older brother named Walter after their father, but the family nicknamed his Steaks. When he was a baby, he used a teething ring as a steak. It was while Big Moon was eating his steak and potato dinner. He had Walter Jr on his lap. Quickly the baby grabbed the steak off the plate, put it in his mouth, and gummed it; the pressure felt good on his gums, and he enjoyed the taste.

Harlem is a pretty woman. She stands at an even five feet, five inches. She wears her hair in dreadlocks, long dreadlocks that she pins in a bun, and ties a colorful head scarf around her bun. She has large moon-shaped brown eyes and dimples. Her rich brown skin looks sparkles looks cooper in the sunshine. She has a cool gentle nature; very seldom does she get upset.

Harlem always wanted to have her own coffee house. She loves the atmosphere of sitting in a coffee house with her friends and family, drinking hot coffee, and eating a sweet treat. Harlem loves coffee, especially flavored coffees. Whenever there was a party or get-together, Harlem didn't serve wine, beer, or any other alcoholic beverages; she would serve her coffees and ask her mother Joyce to make the sweet treats, cookies, cupcakes, muffins, etc.

The idea of starting a coffee shop was just a playful dream that Big Moon and she would share. Instead of having tea parties, when Harlem was a little girl, she would host coffee parties. Big Moon would sit in her bedroom on the floor because he was too big to sit in the little chairs. He and she would sip pretend coffee from her little plastic coffee mug. Joyce would look on smiling and serve the fresh baked cookies.

Big Moon and Joyce always encouraged their children to go for their dreams, but they also taught their children to have good-paying jobs.

"Pay your tithes first, baby," Joyce would instruct. "Pay yourself and always pay your rent and light bill first, and everything will fall into place."

Big Moon and Joyce taught their children morals and values. Seeing the lovely marriage that their parents had, both Steaks and Harlem wanted to get married and have a family.

Steaks got married right after college. He met a nice girl named Lauryn. She was a pretty dark-skinned beauty. Both Steaks and she went to college for business. Lauryn always wanted to have her own interior design company, and Steaks worked in accounting. Steaks and Lauryn had three children; two boys and one girl. Walter III, who they nicked named Little Moon, because when he was born, he looked just like Big Moon. The middle boy, who they named Knight. He happens to be Harlem's favorite because he was born on her birthday, and the baby girl name Queen. Harlem loves her niece and nephews, and they love their Aunt Harlem. Like Steaks, Harlem went to school for business and studied accounting. Big Moon and Joyce were proud of their children. Having a good education and family were goals that many strived for. Although Harlem was genuinely happy, she felt she was missing something. She didn't have the job she wanted. She ended up working in a call center, she was management, but the call center seemed like a dead-end job. The tan-colored walls, the fluorescence light, the windows that didn't open; Harlem became like a zombie. Harlem would talk about it with Joyce and Big Moon over Sunday dinner.

"Live your dreams, baby girl." Big Moon would say.

Harlem would take in a deep breath and nodded her head, not sure what her dream was. She met Stephen at the annual R & B Festival. It was a festival that is held once a year on a weekend in the Caribbean Islands. Harlem, Lauryn, and Harlem's good friends Monique, whom they call Lady Mo, and another friend Sade would attend the festival every year.

This year's festival was particularly important. Stephen's marketing firm was in charge of the advertising and marketing of the event. Stephen Graham was a hard worker. At the time of the festival, Stephen was a young, eager executive setting his goals to be a V.P, if not a marketing firm partner, Mitchel Berry, and Hutch. He was a hard worker, working long hours. Stephen managed to convince his manager to allow him to be in charge of the promotion and marketing for the R & B Festival. Stephen had a plan to make sure that this festival would be the best. With R & B singers and performers' line-up, Stephen knew that the turnout would be the biggest festival the Caribbean Island would see.

It was hot that particular summer, but the humidity, the blazing sun did stop the fun at the R & B festival. Thousands of people showed up to party the weekend away, including Harlem, Lauryn, two of their good friends, Sade, and their good friend, Monique, whom the girls affectionately call Lady Mo. The girls looked forward to their weekend away, especially Lauryn. Steaks would watch the kids so she can let her hair down and dance with the people to music and get baptized in the heat. Harlem, Sade, and

Lady Mo would enjoy the festival because it gave them the freedom they needed to get away from the call center. Stephen looked at the sea of people dancing and singing along with their favorite artists; he enjoyed the show. He led the executive marketing team to promote this event. He coordinated with the performers and their managers to know their needs during their time at the festival. He sat at the bar nursing a beer when Harlem and Lady Mo walked to the bar.

"Yes!" Lady Mo said, dancing. "Girl!"

Harlem laughed at her friend as she danced at the bar. Harlem glanced at the bartender and Stephen as they watched and enjoyed Lady Mo's carefree demeanor.

"You ladies enjoying yourself?" the bartender asked.

"Yes," Harlem said smiling.

"What can I get you to drink?" the bartender asked.

"Two beers," Lady Mo said.

"Just a glass of ice water for me," Harlem said.

"Glad you're enjoying yourself," Stephen said.

"This year's event is well put together!" Harlem said, fanning herself. "Humid, but I'm enjoying this year's line-up."

The bartender placed two frosted mugs on the bar. He gave Harlem a bottle of Aquafina and Lady Mo an opened bottle of Yuengling. The two ladies drank their beverage and let out a sigh.

"Glad you're enjoying the show," Stephen said, smiling and feeling proud.

"See brotha, relax," the bartender said to Stephen.

Harlem and Lady Mo looked at the two men then the bartender smiled.

"Stephen's marketing firm organized this year's festival." The bartender informed.

Harlem smiled at Stephen.

"Real nice," Harlem said to Stephen, sipping her water.

Stephen nodded his head modestly.

"Thank you," he said.

The Road That Life Turns

Stephen thought Harlem was beautiful. She had dark brown skin, and her dreadlocks were pinned into a bun with a red scarf around the bun. She wore an off-the-shoulder red top with a pair of white, wide-legged pants. She was beautiful. He knew at that moment he was going to marry her.

"Stephen Graham." Stephen introduces himself.

He held out his hand for Harlem and Lady Mo to shake, especially Harlem. The ladies shake his hand. Lady Mo could see that Stephen had eyes for Harlem.

"My name is Harlem," Harlem introduced. "and this is my friend Monique."

"Harlem," Stephen said. "Like New York."

"Yes," Harlem said with a grin.

"That's an unusual name," Stephen said, grinned at Harlem.

"Her family is known for their unusual names." Lady Mo joked. "Her brother's name is Steaks, her father's name is Big Moon."

"Mo-," Harlem admonished, smiling.

"Sorry, girl," Lady Mo said.

"Those are nicknames," Harlem said, smiling.

Stephen nodded his head.

"What do you do?" Stephen asked.

Harlem shrugged her shoulders.

"I'm an accounting manager at an insurance company," Harlem answered.

"Where are you ladies from?"

"Atlanta," Lady Mo answered.

"Me too," Stephen smiled.

"Ladies and gentlemen!" said the announcer.

Lady Mo and Harlem put their attention to the speaker in the bar.

"Get ready for the smooth sounds of Eli Jones!"

"Girl!" Lady Mo shouted.

Lady Mo was about to put money down on the bar to cover her beer; Stephen waved his hand.

"I got the tab," Stephen said.

"Thank you." Lady Mo said.

The ladies put their glasses on the bar, and left Stephen and the bartender to enjoy the rest of the concert. Stephen watched as the girls disappeared into the crowd.

STEAKS ENTERS CAFÉ MOON; he smiles and waves at the staff, Candice, and Mark, assisting the customers. Steaks looks around Café Moon. He is proud of his little sister. Café Moon has been successful since the opening.

"Morning, Mommy." Steaks greet his mother.

Steaks greets his mother was a kiss on the cheek.

"Morning, baby." Joyce greets smiling.

"Here you go, Steaks," Candice says, smiling, giving him a large coffee.

"Thanks, Candice," Steaks says, "Where is Harlem?"

"In her office," Joyce answers.

"How is she doing?" Steaks asked.

"You know her," Joyce begins, whipping down a table. "She won't say too much."

Steaks let out a sigh.

"Is she talking?" Steaks asks.

"She doesn't seem distant." Joyce answers.

Steaks looks off into the distance and then shakes his head.

"What happened?" Steaks asked.

He follows his mother around the café as she whips the tables clean. Joyce shrugs her shoulders as she sprays the table down with cleanser.

"I don't know, Steaks. She just told me that she and Stephen are divorcing."

Mark, and Candice slowly creep toward Joyce and Steaks. Joyce looks at them scornfully.

"Miss Joyce-," Candice begins.

Joyce interrupts Candice by holding her hand up at Candice, indicating for her to hush. Candice knows that sign; she immediately stops talking.

"Family business," Joyce scolds.

"Miss Joyce, all due respect, we are family. Harlem has taken care of Mark and me. We care about her too."

Joyce smiles at their devotion. She nodded her head, accepting their curiosity.

"Let Harlem inform you then; it's not my business to tell."

Joyce's eyes shift towards the back. Harlem is approaching from the back, caring her coffee mug. Joyce clears her throat, which is another sign for them to get back to work. Immediately Mark and Candice scatters to return to work or to make it look like they been working hard. Mark takes the cloth and spray bottle from Joyce and whips the empty tables, and Candice scurries to make a fresh coffee pot.

"Hey, Steaks," Harlem says, smiling.

"What's up, Sis." Steaks replies. "Everything okay?"

"Yes," she answers, smiling.

Harlem takes in a deep breath, her eyes scan the room, and sees Mark and Candice attempt to appear busy. She chuckles.

"I'm fine." She says again. "Stephen and I will be fine."

"What happened?" Steaks questioned.

"Nothing," Harlem answers.

"You don't get divorced over nothing." Steaks states.

"Steaks, I'm working," Harlem said. "I don't want to discuss anything right now,"

Harlem hands Mark her coffee mug and then walks to the chalkboard in front of the counter; she writes the name of the newest coffee blend. Harlem looks to Mark and Candice.

"I need you two to push this," she says to them.

Mark and Candice nod their heads. Harlem turns around to find her mother and brother looking at her. The fact that they are here is comforting, but now is not the time to dwell on the issues. What happened? Who fault is it? She looks at Steaks; he has the look that says:

"Do I need to beat need to beat Stephen up?"

"It was amicable," Harlem said. "Stephen and I are both divorcing,"

"Why?" Steaks asked.

"What do you mean why?" Harlem questions. "Think Steaks, we just didn't work. There was never a Stephen and Harlem or Starlem."

Steaks chuckles at the term Harlem used to brand a couple.

"What about counseling?" Steaks suggested.

Harlem shakes her head;

"We're past counseling. It's time to go our separate ways."

Harlem, Steaks, and Joyce noticed that business was starting to pick up at Café Moon, the morning rush was over, and now it's time for the pre-lunch rush. A line is forming at the register, and several customers have taking seats to look over a takeout menu. Harlem closes her eyes and inhales the smell of fresh coffee; she smells the fresh smell of cinnamon and sugar.

$$\text{\Large ◖}$$

Harlem sat at the table Saturday morning, sipping a peppermint mocha. While waiting for her friend Sade, she sat outside on the deck at the coffee shop, enjoying the baptism of the morning sun. While waiting, she read over the newsfeed on the Yahoo app on her cell phone

"Good morning," said a voice.

Harlem looks up from her cell phone and saw a familiar face. He saw in her eyes she was trying to remember where she saw him from. What was familiar about him?

"Stephen Graham," Stephen said, extending his hand. "Is Harlem, right?"

"Yes," Harlem said, being polite but still not remembering.

"The R & B Fest," Stephen said. "The marketing firm that I worked for sphere headed the concert. I met you and your friend and the cocktail bar."

"Oh yes," Harlem said, smiling, now really remembering him.

Stephen was relieved. Suddenly he was at a loss for words. He didn't know what to say. He had a grin on his face, hoping to hide his embarrassment. Her pretty eyes looking at him, wondering what he wanted.

"I was just surprised to see you. I didn't know you live on this side of town."

"Oh, okay," Harlem said.

Stephen, still nervous, takes in a deep breath.

"Would you like to get a cup of coffee somewhere?"

Harlem holds up her mocha. Stephen chuckles and looks away. He closes his eyes real tight and pieces his lips together. Harlem laughs.

"I'm sorry." He said. "I am a bit off my game. I specifically remember how beautiful you looked at the festival. You are just as beautiful now."

"Thank you," Harlem said bashfully.

"Can I meet you here next Saturday morning for coffee?" Stephen asked.

Harlem grinned and sipped her coffee.

"I am usually here Saturday morning with my friend; we have breakfast," Harlem said. "How about we meet here for lunch. I know better than to interfere with girl's time."

"Okay," Harlem said with a chuckle.

Feeling more confident, Stephen smiles and walks away. Just as he leaves, Sade approaches the table with her coffee and pastry in her hand. She had a wide smile.

"What's going on here?" Sade asked, smiling as she sat down.

"Nothing," Harlem said evasively.

"Doesn't look like nothing," Sade said.

Harlem rolled her eyes.

"He was at that R & B Fest. Lady Mo and I struck up conversation at the cocktail bar. He was surprised to see me here."

"And," Sade pressed.

"And, he asked if we can go out to lunch," Harlem answers with a grin. "It was nothing. We're meeting here next Saturday afternoon."

"Why are you meeting here?" Sade asked, with a smirk, taking a bite out of her cookie.

Harlem shrugged her shoulders.

"Anyway! How was your week?" Harlem asked.

"Work is work."

Sade leans her head back and lets out a sigh.

"I am sick of call centers."

"What are we going to do?" Harlem asked with a chuckle.

"Find me a rich man." Sade jokes. "Plus, this coffee is overpriced, and this cookie is too weak. Why do we keep coming here?"

"Because the coffee is good, and they let us sit here as long as we want," Harlem said.

Sade scuffed.

"What's the problem, Sade?" Harlem asked.

"I need a man; I need some money." Sade laughed. "*When* are you going to stop pissing around and open up your own coffee house. So I can have a free cup?!"

Harlem laughed.

The Road That Life Turns

The idea of owning her own coffee house was something that Harlem always gave thought to, but at the time didn't act on it.

HARLEM ARRIVES HOME TO her apartment. Stephen is sitting on the balcony smoking a cigar. He hasn't moved out yet. There is no rush. There was no; "Get your stuff and get out!" It was, "I'll be out by the end of the month."

Stephen decided to let Harlem keep the apartment, considering it close to Café Moon, and she has to be at the café by five am. He is just as numb as Harlem is regarding the divorce. To him, there is no reason. There has been no infidelity, no abuse of any kind—just a bad season, a season that phased out.

Harlem used to smile and greet him whenever Stephen came home from work; he smiled at her, both of them happy to see each other, but for three years, no one smiled at anyone and no one greeted each other whenever they came home from work. There is no,
"How was your day?" Life had become; "I'm stuck at work. I'll call you later."

Stephen worked hard to be the Vice President at the aid agency, excelling in deals after deals. He promised Harlem after this deal falls through, we'll go on that vacation." Or the promise of, "I'll be home soon."

Stephen's goal was so she didn't have to work. Stephen wanted to give her everything.

On that Saturday afternoon, Harlem met Stephen at the coffee house as planned. At first, she had her Saturday morning breakfast with Sade.

"You nervous?" Sade asked

"No, " Harlem answered, shaking her head. "We're just having coffee."

"I know," Sade said, smiling. "It's been a long time since you had coffee with someone."

Harlem rolled her eyes.

"How was your work week?" Harlem asked.

"Don't how's your work week with me," Sade said. "What's going on with your job?"

"New claims to process, verifying coordination of benefits," Harlem said, teasing her enthusiasm.

"We both need stimulation," Sade said. "Maybe this guy, this date-,"

"It's' not a date," Harlem said. "It's just coffee."

Stephen entered the coffee shop. He saw Harlem and her friend laughing at the table. Both ladies smiled as he approached the table, carrying two cups of coffee in his hand, one black, the other a peppermint mocha.

"Hi," Harlem said, standing up.

"Hello," Stephen said, smiling.

Sade also stood up. She grabbed her purse in preparation to leave.

"Hi, I'm Sade." She introduced herself.

"I'm Stephen."

"Nice to meet you," Sade said. "Harlem, call me later."

Sade left. Harlem looked at Stephen. He smiled and handed her the cup of coffee that he brought her.

"This is for you."

Harlem took the coffee, sipped it, and closed her eyes, enjoying the sweet taste of the peppermint.

"How did you know?" Harlem asked, smiling, taking another sip.

"I asked the barmaid behind the counter what you usually get."

"Thank you," Harlem said, smiling.

Together, Harem and Stephen sat down.

"So every Saturday, you and your friend come here?" Stephen asked.

Harlem nodded his head.

"Yes, my friend Sade and I come here every Saturday morning. We kind of unwind from work. We kind of unwind from our workweek, get our nails done, go shopping."

"Are all your Saturday mornings full?" Stephen asked.

"No, it all depends on the mood she and I are in," Harlem said. "Saturday evening, my family, my brother, mom, and dad and I meet up for a family dinner."

"What do you do for a living?"

"I am a manager for an insurance company, customer service. Nothing glamorous as working for an aid agency." Harlem teased.

"My job is not glamorous," Stephen said, smiling.

"No," Harlem playfully interrogates. "You do photoshoots, create commercials shoots, meet models, travel."

"Okay, okay, there is some glamor," Stephen admits, with a chuckle.

Harlem laughs.

"What do you do in your spare time?" Harlem asked.

"The normal guy stuff. Golf, play ball with the boys." Stephen answered. "You."

"The same, but girl stuff," she smiles. "Shop or spend time with my family. Any siblings?"

"Yeah, two brothers, Sam and Seth."

"All S'," Harlem said.

"I have a brother; we call him Steaks."

"I remember your friend talking about that; why Steaks?" Stephen asked.

"A childhood name." Harlem answers.

"What about the name Harlem?" Stephen asked. "Any special meaning?"

"Not sure why. My father just liked the name."

Stephen sipped his coffee.

They talked at the coffee house for hours. Neither of them wanting to leave. Harlem listened as Stephen talked about his goals regarding the aid agency. He wanted to be the president at the agency. He talked about how much he loved marketing. He loved coming up with ideas for each new campaign, from coffee, to toilet paper, to a fashion designer's new clothing line, restaurants.

"What's your favorite?" Harlem asked.

Stephen shrugged his shoulders.

"I don't I have a favorite campaign," Stephen answered. "I just love coming up with ideas; I love overseeing the ideas. I love seeing the final product, like that R & B Fest. Watching the people dance to the entertainer, enjoying the food, hearing how everyone enjoyed their hotel, the island, everything. The final results, knowing that was my name that handled everything."

"What do your parents think of your success?" Harlem asked.

"My folks are gone," Stephen said.

"My mom died when I was young, and my father a year after college."

Harlem shook her head.

"I'm sorry." She said. "I don't know what I would do if I lost both of my parents."

"My brothers and I do alright," Stephen said.

Stephen looked at his watch.

"We've been here for a while. Would you like to get something to eat?"

"HARLEM!" Stephen said her name, calling her from her thoughts.

She sits on the couch; her laptop is opened with her excel spreadsheet in view. Harlem lost focus. She looks at Stephen.

"Did you eat?" he asked. "I'm going to order a pizza."

"Um, no, no, thank you." She replies.

Stephen nods his head and walks away to order his food. He can't understand how calm and cool she is right now. He can't believe how cool and calm he is. He shakes his head as he calls the pizzeria.

The Road That Life Turns

"Hi, I like to order for a delivery." He said. "Large pepperoni. Yes, Wilson St, fourth floor… yes, cash…, thank you."

Stephen hangs up the phone and walks back to the balcony.

What happened? He had liked her from the start. It wasn't long before he fell in love with her. He still likes her, still loves her, but her silence is deafening. There is no talking, no laughing. The light in her eyes are dim. Harlem doesn't smile at him anymore. She is pleasant, just not happy. There are no children to distract them, just jobs and businesses.

O

On their date, their first date, Stephen and Harlem enjoyed a nice late lunch and took a walk along the park. Everything seemed pleasant, a pleasant park, a cool breeze, and a full moon in the sky. Harlem and Stephen enjoyed this time. They talked about everything, their hopes and dreams, and desires. They talked about sports and politics. Stephen noticed Harlem's fondness for coffee houses. She pointed out some of her favorites in the city. Stephen loved looking at her bright and pretty smile. He saw that she had hopes and desires for a simple life, nothing major, nothing luxurious. As beautiful as Harlem was, she had a charming modesty about her.

From Stephen's experience, he dated girls that once they found out that he was one of the top exec at the aid agency, the women wanted to be a part of his glamorous life. They wanted to be on his arm at the dinners with new clients or at the office holiday parties. Stephen had dated beautiful and intelligent women, who were well known in society, had a good network of friends and businessmen and women that would help enhance Stephen to the executive platform that he was striving for. However, with Harlem, he saw that Harlem would love to be on his arm, but just to be by his side and support him, not to gain a social network for herself.

"What is with you and coffee houses?"

"I don't know; I love the intimacy of the coffee house; just you and the cup, ya know. There is a type of serenity, a sense of peace and quiet. I love how it's a cool place to meet up with friends and unwind."

Harlem and Stephen walked into another coffee house. They order a cup of decaffeinated coffee and sat down at an empty table; this time, they sat next to each other, unlike earlier when they sat across from each other.

"A glass of wine or beer-,"

"It's more than that." Harlem interrupts. "When I drink my mocha, it's warm and relaxing. When I was a little girl would have coffee parties, not tea parties, but coffee parties. My mom would make the cookies or muffins. My father and I would sip the imaginary coffee and eat the pastries."

"You're close with your family?" Stephen stated, smiling.

"Yes," Harlem nodded her head. "Steaks and I are very close, and our parents are so cool."

Harlem looked around and noticed that the coffee bar was near closing.

"It's getting late." She said.

"Okay," Stephen said.

Stephen drove Harlem to the location they met. Stephen walked her to her car.

"I enjoyed myself," Stephen said. "Can I see you again?"

"I would like that," Harlem said, smiling.

Stephen and Harlem both pulled out their cell phones and exchanged phone numbers. As Stephen put his cell phone in his pocket and Harlem fiddled with her car keys, they looked at each other nervously, not knowing if there should be a good night kiss. However, Stephen leaned forward and kissed Harlem on the cheek. Harlem grinned; she looked up at Stephen.

"I'll call you later in the week." He said.

The Road That Life Turns

"Okay," Harlem said.
Stephen stood by to watch Harlem get in the car, put on her seat belt, start the engine, and drive off. There was a full moon that night, and to him, that a good sign. He took in a deep breath and knew at that moment that she was going to be his wife.

Stephen and Harlem got married a year later. During that year, they were always together. After a month of dating, they met each other's families. Steaks and Big Moon met Stephen and liked him immediately. He was a career man, and they liked that for Harlem. Both men knew that Harlem would be well taken care of. Stephen had no problem joining Harlem to have family dinner on Saturdays. Joyce thought Stephen was a perfect gentleman, just like her husband. She thought of the pretty chocolate-colored grandbabies that Stephen and Harlem would give her, to add to the grandbabies that Steaks and Lauryn has given her. Stephen's brothers liked Harlem. She was cool, laid back, and calm. Her relaxed demeanor made it easy to talk to her. Conversations were pushed or forced, just a natural flow.

At the office parties, the parties for the clients, or celebrating a campaign, Harlem charmed all of the big corporate men and women. Stephen smiled as Harlem got along with his bosses and their wives. It was if she fit in, she didn't over smile or over talk. Harlem didn't have a motive to increase her social network, and she just enjoyed being on Stephen's arm. Her modesty was deserving of the glamorous life. Stephen had the money to give her the glamorous life. As he climbed the cooperate later, he knew that he had and will have the money for Harlem to live the life like his boss' wives.

The night when Stephen proposed, they sat on the bench at a local park. The fall season had started to settle in; although it was cool outside, they loved looking at the fall leaves' beautiful colors. There was a full moon in the sky, and the clouds slowly moved, making the moon and the clouds look almost 3D. It was a beautiful image, and he could see that Harlem was enjoying the scenery. This was a perfect setting to propose. Stephen presented Harlem with a small ring box with a large princess cut diamond inside. Harlem looked at the beautiful see-through diamond in shocked. She looked at Stephen; he was smiling.

"You had to know that this was coming." He said. "We talked about possibilities."

"Yes, we talked about what-ifs," Harlem said. "but,"

"But what?" Stephen asked with a chuckle.

Harlem shrugged.

"I just didn't think it would happen so soon. I was, am, enjoying where we are." She said, smiling.

"So let's go further," Stephen said, smiling. "Be my wife."

Harlem nodded her head, smiling.

"Yes." She said.

Stephen slipped the beautiful ring on her finger, and they shared a passionate kiss.

"After we are married, you don't have to work," Stephen said. "You can come out of that boring call center and stay at home if you want."

She liked the idea of being a stay-at-home wife. Joyce was a stay-at-home wife. Harlem remembers how well her mother managed the household, made sure dinner was ready, clean clothes, and how she did special things with her and Steaks. Harlem loved the idea of being available for her children, the children that she and Stephen would have.

The wedding was beautiful. A beautiful neo-soul themed wedding on the beach. Harlem wanted things simple. There is no bridal party, just friends and family on the beach watching two people in love get married at sunset. Harlem looked like a beautiful African goddess. She wore her long dreadlock down with a few cowrie shells placed variously in her hair. She wore a long white dress strapless white dress; her chocolate brown skin sparkled under the sun. Stephen wore a black tuxedo, white the white shirt opened at the collar to make him appear more relaxed; he too was barefoot. As they held hands exchanging vows, Stephen smiled at her. Under the sunset, Harlem was so beautiful; he didn't stop the tears from falling down his eyes. Harlem smiled at Stephen; he was handsome.

They honeymoon on a tropical island. Harlem enjoyed the white sand between her toes. Life had no ceiling; life had no limits or boundaries. She was a married woman. Married to a good man and now will live the good life. As she stood at the edge of the beach and the water crashed against her feet, Harlem looked out at the ocean and saw there were no walls. She loved the fact that she doesn't have to go to work when she goes back to the states. She will go to her penthouse apartment, sit on the balcony and sip coffee, watching the sun rise. She will not be pressed to be morning rush hour traffic. Stephen will go to work, or he can work from home. Harlem imaged having that morning coffee with her mother, now that they are housewives. Joyce would give Harlem advice on how to be a perfect wife. Harlem imagined Stephen smiling like Big Moon, happy with his life.

As Stephen and Harlem settled into their apartment, Harlem happily adjusted to being a housewife. She remembers watching Joyce do the laundry on certain days and Harlem remembers that her mother dusted first thing in the morning after breakfast. However, by noon, housework was done, and there was nothing left to do. Her friends had full-time jobs so they were at work, so she couldn't just call them in the middle of the day. The wives of Stephen's colleagues seemed fickled, catty, and arrogant. They spent their days either shopping, getting some kind of injections for their looks, or planning some kind of social event. Some of the women assisted in their children's school, planning fundraisers; they were "soccer moms," but Harlem didn't have children.

"You want to start having kids?" Stephen asked.

They were eating dinner one night; Harlem shrugged her shoulders. She wasn't sure if she wanted kids now or not. They were now married for almost a year.

Kids will be nice, but now; not so sure. Harlem took in a deep breath.

"I'm bored." She confessed. "I can shop until I drop but I don't want to spend your money-,"

"Our money," Stephen corrected.

"You know what I mean," Harlem said. "Your co-workers' wives are so-,"

Stephen chuckled.

"You're right," Stephen said. "That is one of the reasons why I fell in love with you; you weren't superficial."

"I am not sure if they are wives or reality T.V., stars. They have wigs and weaves, eyelashes and injections in the butts."

"Do you want to go back to work?" Stephen asked.

Harlem shook her head.

"I got a taste of freedom." She joked. "I don't know what I want to do. I'm sorry for being so indecisive."

Stephen chuckled; he finished eating, swallowed the last drop of wine, and quickly stands up. He grabbed his plate and wine glass. Quickly he rinsed them both and placed them in the dishwasher.

"I'm going to work on some files," Stephen said.

He kissed Harlem on the top of her head and left her alone at the table. There is more to being Mrs. Stephen Graham. She looked at her wedding ring, a nice princess cut diamond, and a diamond wedding band. For the first time since Stephen and she meet, she feels alone and useless.

2

"I NEED A FRESH order of white almond cupcakes with buttercream icing." Harlem called out to the bakers at Café Moon.

Joyce, who is the head chef, nods her head with a smile. She is so proud of Harlem. Joyce looks up at a ceiling, smiling at Big Moon.

You be so proud. Joyce says in her heart.

HARLEM AND STEPHEN BEEN married for almost two years when Big Moon grew ill. For two years, Harlem, Steaks, and Joyce took care of him. Cancer had taken control of his body, forcing him to be bedridden. Although cancer had his body, cancer did not have his spirit. He would lay or sit in bed with his family, play cards, watch T.V.; he was happy to have his family rally around for him. Seeing her father smile and laugh although he was sick gave Harlem hope that he would bet cancer. No matter the amount of chemotherapy he got, Big Moon always had a smile on his face. He was always in good spirits.

One particular day, a Wednesday afternoon, Big Moon laid in his bed with the television on to some kind of CNN television program. Steaks and Harlem sat on opposite sides of Big Moon.

"Steaks," Big Moon said.

"Sir," Steaks replied.

"Bring your mother in here." Big Moon requested.

"I'm here," Joyce said, coming in from the living room.

Joyce approached the bed. Steaks stood up to allow his mother to sit next to Big Moon.

Big Moon took in a deep breath. He looked at Joyce, the love of his life. Her pretty caramel skin was soft. Joyce wore her dark hair in pin curls. She smiled at Big Moon. Joyce can see that he is tired. Big Moon smiled back. He is so appreciative of her and of their love.

"I love you." Big Moon said to Joyce.

There was power behind that; I love you. Joyce and Big Moon always told each other that they love one another, but this time, the I love you, was different. Joyce took in a deep breath, tears fill her eyes and fell down her cheeks. Steaks and Harlem's eyes also fill up with tears.

"Big Moon," Harlem said, as tears fell down her cheeks.

Big Moon looked at his children and he grinned.

"You two." Big Moon begins. "I am so proud of you."

"Big Moon," Steaks said, he grinned at his father. "Come on, relax; we're here."

Big Moon grinned. He nodded his head.

"Steaks, my son, remember what I taught you. Love your family. Harlem, baby."

Harlem shook her head, fighting the urge to sob. She knew that her father was saying good-bye. She didn't want to hear goodbye.

"Big Moon, no, please." Harlem cried.

"Baby girl." Big Moon said with a smile. "Remember, I love you. Follow your dreams."

Big Moon's eyes shift to look at Joyce. Her face wet with tears.

"I am truly a blessed man because of you." Big Moon said.

Joyce leaned forward and kissed Big Moon on the lips.

"Go to sleep, my love."

Big Moon closed his eyes and took in a deep breath, and slowly exhaled. He was gone. Harlem cried out.

"Big Moon!" she screamed. "Mommy, wake him up!"

Steaks grabbed his sister in his arms, trying to restrain her.

"Mommy please!" Harlem screams. "BIG MOON!!!"

"Harlem, baby, come on." Steaks comforted. "We'll be okay."

The Road That Life Turns

Harlem sobbed in her brother's arms. Steaks held on to his sister tightly and he too cried. Joyce sat at the bedside next to her husband. With her head buried in her hands, she sobbed.

HARLEM WAS QUIET AND subdued during the planning of the funeral. She tried to interact with friends and family, but her heart was broken. Stephen tried to help; he taken time away from work to be there for her and to help out in anyway he could for the family.

That night after the funeral, Harlem sat on the balcony, the air warm and still. The sky is dark, no full moon in the sky, no half moon or even a crescent moon. Stephen sat next to Harlem.

"There is no moon." She said softly.

Stephen looked up at the heavens. He didn't know what to say.

A week after Big Moon's funeral, there was the reading of the will. Joyce, Steaks, and Lauryn sat in the law office. The lawyer read over the will.

"I Walter Green Sr., of sound body and mind leaving the following to my immediate family. My wife of thirty-five years, Joyce...,"

The lawyer proceed to read what Big Moon willed to his wife. There was a gasp in the room. No one knew that Big Moon had such a fortune, leaving so much to his wife. The lawyer continued.

"To my son, Walter Green Jr., and his wife, Lauryn..,"

The lawyer proceeded to inform of the heirlooms' valuable items that Steaks and Lauryn would cherish. Again, gasp filled the room. Lauryn dabbed the tears from the corner of her eyes. Thankful for Big Moon to consider her in his will. She had always loved Big Moon as if he was her own father, and Big Moon had loved her as one of his children.

"Last but not least, my baby girl, Harlem. I leave you-,"

The lawyer read the value of money that Big Moon left Harlem. Like for Joyce, everyone gasped at the large value of money Big Moon left Harlem. However, the amount of money did not impress Harlem. Without out Big Moon, what he left her meant nothing.

"Stephen Graham, my son-in-law," the lawyer continued.

Stephen sat up shocked that the lawyer called out his name. The lawyer read what Big Moon left Stephen. Stephen's heart melted at the idea that Big Moon left him some precious value.

After the reading, the family went to Harlem's favorite coffee house, the same coffee house that Stephen and Harlem had their first date. They sat and reminisced on Big Moon.

"He was an awesome man," Stephen said.

"Thanks brother." Steaks said to Stephen.

Steaks looked at Harlem. She still looked sad and heartbroken, there was no laughter in his eyes.

"Har," Steaks said. "You good?'

"Yeah," Harlem answered. "I'm good."

Later that night, Harlem sat on the balcony. The air was still warm and humid, and again, no moon in the sky. Stephen joined Harlem.

"Your dad gave me his blessing to marry you because I made you smile," Stephen said. "He said, 'Keep her smiling.' Baby, what can I do to make you smile again? Don't let me break the promise I made to your dad."

Little did Stephen noticed, Harlem had stopped smiling a year after they were married. Stephen spent less time at home and more time at the office, working on aid campaign after aid campaign. Stephen was on locations; he was on photo shoots, he worked late at the office working on contracts and storyboards. He was climbing the cooperate later, leaving Harlem at home in their well-furnished penthouse or going to social events alone. Dinner parties with friends and family she went to them without Stephen.

The Road That Life Turns

"Working late," she said smiling. "A big campaign. One of the biggest ones yet."

Big Moon sensed something was wrong, but he didn't want to pry. He wanted to question, "Where is your husband?" but Big Moon didn't ask. He didn't see any disdain in Harlem's eyes. He didn't see any bruising on hiding of the skin. She wasn't wearing long sleeves in the summer. So maybe Stephen was busy, he will make things up with Harlem. With the life style that they live, Stephen needed to work. Big Moon noticed the diamond earrings and fancy clothes that Harlem wore. So again, he didn't ask any questions.

IT WAS THREE IN the morning. Big Moon had been dead for two years. Harlem slept soundly in the bed, and Stephen slept soundly beside her when she heard her name being called.

"Harlem." Said a voice softly. "Harlem."

Harlem thought it was Stephen talking in his sleep. She sat up to shake Stephen, but she saw that he was in a deep sleep, so it wasn't him calling him.

"Harlem," the voice said again.

She knew that voice. Quickly, she climbed out of bed and walked around the penthouse looking the person connected to the voice. She finds him sitting on the sofa.

"Big Moon." She said, trying not to scream.

"Baby girl." He said, smiling.

"Am I dead?" Harlem asked.

"No." he chuckled. "Come sit next to me."

Big Moon tapped the soft cushion next to him. Quickly she approaches the seat next to her father and sits down next to him. He wraps his arms around her, and she rested her head on his large chest.

"You come back." She asked.

Big Moon shakes his head.

"No, baby girl." He answered. "I come to see about my baby and why you have been so so sad."

"I miss you." She said, sitting up. "I don't want this. I don't want this life without you."

"Baby girl, you have to live." Big Moon said. "I'm in a better place."

Harlem shrugged her shoulders.

"I want you here with me." She pouted.

"Live your dreams." Big Moon encouraged.

"I don't have any dreams," Harlem said.

"Yes you do, baby." Big Moon said. "That coffee house."

Harlem chuckled.

"That was our thing." She said.

"It was, but now it can be your thing." Big Moon said. "Start your own coffee house; that was always your dream."

The word dream echoed in Harlem's ear, causing her to wake up. Harlem sits up in bed and looks around. It's four in the morning. Quickly she climbs out of bed and runs into the living room, and she turns the light on. Big Moon is not there, but before her heart can break, glances at the bay window and gasp at the sight. There is a large full moon in the sky. Harlem quickly walked to the window and stared at the full moon; tears welled up in her eyes.

"I love you, Big Moon."

Harlem went in to the kitchen and a pot of coffee. While the coffee brewed, Harlem went into the small office, grabbed a few sheets of paper and a pen and returned to the kitchen. She fixed herself a coffee cup and sat down at the table and began writing ideas for her coffee house.

STEPHEN FOUND HER IN the kitchen a few hours later. He was dressed and ready for work.

"Good morning," Stephen said. "You're up early."

Harlem looked up smiling.

"I saw Big Moon in my dream." He said. "He told me to live my dream. A coffee house. I'm going to take that money he left me to start my own coffee house."

"Really," Stephen said, pouring a cup of coffee.

"Yes," Harlem said, smiling. "Café Moon. I'm going to call it Café Moon."

Stephen grinned. He sat down beside Harlem and looked at the notes that she wrote down for her coffee house.

"This is a lot, Harlem." He said.

"I know, but I got Big Moon's blessing. I saw a full moon last night."

"There was no moon last night," Stephen said.

"There was, Stephen. I saw it this morning."

Stephen didn't want to argue about a full moon. He smiled at Harlem. He kissed her on top of the head.

"I gotta go." He said. "We'll talk more when I get home."

Stephen left, leaving Harlem behind with her coffee and her notes. Harlem called Joyce and Steaks and they came to the penthouse to celebrate with Harlem coming out of her depression.

"I'll bake all the pastries." Joyce volunteered. "I'll bake everything."

"Anything you need, sis." Steaks said, smiling.

3

STEAKS WALKS INTO MITCHELL, Barry ad Hutch Ad Agency. He gets on the elevator and rode it to the twenty-seventh floor, Stephen's floor. Steaks stepped off the elevator and approaches the desk and smiles at the pretty receptionist.

"Hi Walter." She says smiling.

"Hi LaTanya." Steaks said, smiling back. "Is Stephen in?"

"Yes." She answered. "Go right on in."

Steaks likes the perks of being the senior executive's brother-in-law. Steaks knocks and then walks in finding Stephen was pacing the floor talking with two fellow associates as they sat in the office discussing the plans regarding a campaign. Stephen is somewhat startled to see Steaks at his office.

"Steaks!" Stephen said, smiling. "I mean, Walter."

"Stephen." Steaks said, smiling. "Can I talk to you?"

"I'm in a middle of a meeting," Stephen said.

Stephen knows why Steaks is at his office. He wants to speak with him about Harlem. Stephen can see the over protective big brother in Steaks' eyes. Stephen can also see that Steaks isn't going anywhere."

"Gentlemen, let's break," Stephen said. "Fifteen minutes."

The two colleagues were relived to be excused. They quickly get up and walk out of the office, nodding respectfully. Steaks sits down in the chair in front of Stephen's desk.

"What's up?" Stephen asks.

"What's going on with you and my sister?" Steaks asked.

Stephen shakes his head.

"Just not working out." Stephen answers. "Your sister and I are going down two different roads."

"Why?" Steaks ask.

"What do you mean why?" Steaks replies. "Ever since she opened that coffee shop. She doesn't want to spend time with me. She doesn't want to be at home anymore, she won't go to any of the office parties. I come home, she is not there."

"Have you told her how you felt?"

"Yes," Stephen said. "She said, that coffee shop is what Big Moon told her to do."

"That coffee house is helping her cope with Big Moon's death." Steaks said.

"I get that, my parents are dead, but she is working as if she has to work. I told her she doesn't have to work."

"She is following her dream, Stephen." Steaks said.

"This is not what I signed up for," Stephen said.

"What do you mean?" Steaks asked.

"I want a wife, someone to come home to," Stephen answered. "I make enough money for the both of us."

"Stephen, when are you home?" Steaks said. "You are always working, at this meeting or that meeting."

"That so she doesn't have to work." Stephen said.

Steaks sits back in the chair.

"You know how women are. Maybe she want her own money."

"I never made your sister feel that it was *my* money. It's our money."

"I hear what you're saying," Steaks said.

"She works at that coffee house as if Big Moon is coming back." Stephen said. "When she is home, she is working on the book."

"No, brother, she is living her dream." Steaks said. "Big Moon left her all that money-,"

"You guys knew about that money." Stephen said.

"No," Steaks said. "We knew that my father has some kind of burial plan, but we had no clue that he that lump some of money.

Stephen shrugs his shoulders.

"I know this is your sister, but we haven't had sex in a while." Stephen confessed.

"It's cool." Steaks chuckled. "Why not?"

"I work almost sixteen-hour days. When I get home, she is sleep or not home at all; she's at that coffee house."

"There are some pretty skirts in this building." Stephen jokes.

"Steaks!" Stephen admonishes. "I'm not cheating on your sister."

"Okay, okay, okay." Steaks said. "Is she seeing another?"

"Yes, Café Moon," Stephen answered.

"Why did you get married?" Steaks asked.

"Why not?" Stephen asked. "I reached a certain age, a certain phase in my life, and I wanted a wife. I wanted someone to share it with."

"You're not sharing." Steaks said. "My sister was home by herself in that lavish penthouse trying to host dinner parties without her co-host. The party invitation says; The Grahams invite you, but it's just a Graham hosting."

"Steaks, I have to work to live like we do."

"My sister doesn't want to live the life as some kind of reality housewife." Steaks said. "Our parents didn't raise us to be materialistic. They raised us to be there for each other."

Suddenly Stephen remembers the countless arguments that Harlem and he would have regarding the late hour he would keep at work. She was lonely. Stephen's long hours were questioned numerous of times, his integrity questioned. Is there another woman or women? His drive to be the best, to be on top, was and is driving his wife away. Harlem had begun to spend time with her old friends, who happened to be still single. She resumed her Saturday morning coffee date with Sade.

Stephen was busing working on a new campaign a new project. It was embarrassing to have the perfect husband on paper, but that perfect husband not around. Stephen would be remorseful. He apologize numerous times for standing up Harlem and leaving her there to make up an excuse for him not being there.

Stephen now knows the embarrassment when it came to presentation, the several appearances he had to make alone because she was working at the coffee house.

The Road That Life Turns

Stephen realizes that his ambition cost him his marriage. Stephen looks at Steaks.

"Now what?" Stephen asked.

"Not sure." Steaks stand up.

Suddenly a thunderclap loudly in the sky.

"It's supposed to storm." Steaks said. "I'm going to leave."

Stephen and Steaks stand, and the two shakes hands. Steaks walk out of the office. Stephen sits back down and looks at his cell phone; the last message he sent, he was replying back to Harlem. It was simply an; "Ok." It was a reply from Harlem suggesting that they can divide everything equally. That message was from two days ago. There used to be text messages saying, "I love you." Or "Have a good day," then a kissing emoji next to it.

Both Stephen and Harlem started their day at five in the morning. Coffee is made, but there is no sitting down and eating breakfast together. Stephen can't remember the last time they had dinner together, but what does stick out in his memory is the cool kiss on top of her head, dismissing the conversations when he was finished eating because he needs to get some paperwork done. He shakes his head at what he did.

STEAKS HIT THE BUTTON, which buzzes to Harlem and Stephens' penthouse. Harlem hits the intercom.

"Yes, who is it?" Harlem asked.

"Steaks."

"Come on up," Harlem said, hitting the open button to buzz in her brother.

Harlem unlocks the front door so Steaks can enter once he arrives in the penthouse. She is not in the mood to talk to anyone, especially her brother. She is not in the mood for big brother interference. This is her marriage and her life.

Steaks enters the penthouse. Every time he comes, he is taken back by the splendor of the penthouse. He looks at his sister. Harlem had always been beautiful, but being married to a man with money, she looks more regal. Her eyebrows perfectly arched. Her skin flawless from those expensive skin cleansers and those special facials that one can only get at the spa. She looks like a goddess; she wears her dreadlock down, hanging down her back. He smiles at his sister. She smiles back.

"What's up, lil sis?" Steaks ask.

"Not much big, bro." Harlem answers. "You want something to eat or drink?"

"No," Steaks respectfully declines.

Together they enter the living room. They sit down on the thick comfortable couch with the paisley print cushions. Steaks looks around the living room and admire the beautiful décor: the red cedar wood coffee table and end tables. There is a love seat to match with the couch; the paisley print is navy and emerald. The lamps on the end tables are copper with gold material shade.

"Stephen has you set up real nice." Steak said.

Harlem takes the remote control and turns off the television, the large flat screen that is mounted on the wall.

"What's up?" Harlem asked.

"You." Steaks said. "What is going on?"

"Nothing, Steaks. I told you. Stephen and I are in a different place."

"Did all this start after Big Moon died?"

Harlem shakes her head.

"This has been going on long before Big Moon." Harlem answered. "Stephen is a trophy wife, someone on his arms at the office Christmas party.

Then it was go in his place at those parties. When I did, then expensive furniture came in."

Steaks chuckled by Harlem's joke.

"In the beginning, Stephen and I were always together." Harlem began. "As busy as his schedule was, he always managed to shoot me a text or call me to let me know he was thinking about me. We would have lunch together, morning coffee or dinner."

"Is there someone else?" Steaks ask. "Stephen said no, but I am asking for you?"

"No, Steaks!" Harlem answers, almost offended.

"Okay, okay, Harlem." Steaks said, putting his hands up. "I'm sorry."

"We don't have kids to distract us from the issues. He is not home enough for us to make those babies. At first, I thought it was me. I brought the lingerie, but it wasn't me. I did everything socially, sexually, and financially. Café Moon saved me from self-destruction. Big Moon always encouraged us to follow our dreams. My dream was not to spend it alone in this penthouse palace that Stephen built."

"What about counseling?"

Harlem shrugs her shoulders.

"I'm over it," Harlem said. "I'm over trying to get Stephen to get it! I'm done crying, I'm done looking like Mrs. Graham, smiling like the happy wife when I am unhappy. I look like Harlem, a contestant from the Bachelor. You know the women that are pining after the eligible bachelor. They look desperate and silly on those shows, in their pretty gowns waiting for that man to give them a rose to stay. I tried to host those parties for whatever charity, and I am alone. I don't want to associate with those executives' wive; they are catty, they start trouble, and look like old washed-up models or R & B stars. I can't live like that, Steaks!"

Steaks shake his head. As busy as he is, he always makes time for Lauryn and the kids. He and Lauryn have a date night every week. Harlem or Joyce has to watch the kids so he and Lauryn can go out. She was almost jealous as she watches her brother and sister-in-law get dressed up to go out to dinner or go see a play or some kind of event.

"Sometimes I wonder," Harlem begins. "If I was asking too much. Just have dinner with me. Sit on the balcony with me. Let's take a walk. We are not having sex like a normal married couple; it makes me think as if he even likes me."

Listening to Harlem is breaking Steak's heart. She will always be his baby sister.

"Stephen is not a bad guy." Harlem started off, staring into the distance. "He's just a busy guy. I have such good memories of Mommy, Big Moon, and us together. We watch television or Big Moon and you in the yard playing touch football. Mommy in the kitchen making cookies."

Steak nods his head at the memories.

"I'm sorry, Harlem." Steaks said.

The thunderclaps. Steaks can see from the large bay window that the gray clouds are moving in. Harlem and she nod together about the brewing storm. Together they stand up.

Steaks lean forward and kisses Harlem on top of the head.

"Love you, Sis." Steaks say.

"Love you too," Harlem says. "Be careful going home. Call me to let me know you got home safely."

"Will do."

Harlem walks Steaks to the door, and he leaves. She walks back to the living room, turns the television on, and leans back on the couch, and watches television.

4 THUNDER CLAPS LOUDLY A the rain pours hard and heavy. The sky is dark, gray and the winds blow hard, making the trees waves vigorously. Stephen enters the apartment, soaking wet. Harlem was in the kitchen cooking preparing dinner when she heard him come home.

"Harlem," he calls her name.

She comes from the kitchen she is surprised to him home-early.

"Hey," is all she can say.

"Hi." He replies back.

"I was fixing myself something to eat. Would you like something?" Harlem asks.

"Sure."

Harlem returns to the kitchen. Stephen goes into the spare room where he's been sleeping to change his clothes. He is nervous. He is going to try to convince Harlem to work it out, to work on their marriage. Maybe, just maybe, they can get this hurtle past this road that life turns. All marriages go through rough times; they go through the rain. The idea of him not having Harlem is heavy for him. He loves her. He remembers seeing her beautiful smile at that R & B Festival. She wore those white pants and that red off-the-shoulder top. Her apple-shaped cheekbones make him smile just thinking about it. He remembers her at the coffee house, how she melted as she sipped the peppermint mocha. Her round eyes looking up at him.

How could he have neglected her that way? Then, that year together, they were inseparable. Seeing her smile, seeing her reflecting in his eyes, she hasn't smiled at him in a long time, and as he thinks about that fact, it was long before Big Moon died. He remembers when she had the idea for the coffee house, how excited she was at five in the morning. He remembers how excited she was to share her ideas and plans, and all he did was kiss the top of her head and promise her that they will talk about it more later; they never did

HE FINDS HER IN the kitchen, putting the finishing touches on dinner. She broiled salmon, prepared rice pilaf, and steamed asparagus sauteed in olive oil and garlic.

"Everything looks good," Stephen said.

Harlem grins.

Together they set the table, and within moments, they set down to eat. After a few moments and a few bites, Harlem begins.

"I'm glad you're here," Harlem says.

"Yeah?" Stephen asks.

"Yes, I thought we go over everything that you're taking, and I'm keeping."

Her comment hit Stephen hard. So hard that he coughs. Harlem doesn't notice.

"Harlem," he says her name. "I, ah, I was hoping we talk."

Harlem looks up from her plate at Stephen; she is not sure how to comment.

"About what?" she asked.

"Us," Stephen says.

Harlem sips her wine.

"Harlem,"

"It's too late." She says quickly.

Another hit.

"Is it?" Stephen asked. "We haven't talked-,"

"I've talked." Harlem interrupted. "I've said everything I needed to stay."

Stephen takes in a deep breath. At that moment, he realized that he took her being her for granted. He knows that she has been speaking, but he hasn't been listening. As they sit at the dining room table, he looks at the fixtures, the chandelier, the marble table, the chairs, the expensive and extravagant taste that Stephen thought Harlem would like. He has built a beautiful palace for her, only to leave her here. He looks at her face. The look is a look that he has never seen before; it is a look that says, "I'm done." He can tell that there is no more talking about their marriage and that there is no more trying. She has emotionally checked out.

"We don't have to make this ugly," Harlem said. "We're not ugly people."

Stephen shakes his head.

"I'm not doing this," Stephen said. "I don't want this."

Harlem looked away.

"I know I messed up." He said. "I get it."

Stephen waved his hand at the house, referring to the items.

"I thought this is what will make you happy. I had the money, and you were –are, worth spending every penny on. Because you are a good woman, and you don't spend my money, our money, I want to give you, but all you wanted is me."

Harlem looks at Stephen, not sure if she believes his epiphany.

"Tell me what I need to do," Stephen said.

Before Harlem could speak, they both looked at the window in the dining room. The rain hit the window hard, and the sky was dark, but through the dark sky, there was an image that was familiar and comforting. It was a full moon. Stephen takes in a deep breath and then looks at Harlem. She too, takes in a deep breath and looks at Stephen.

The Road That Life Turns

Made in the USA
Middletown, DE
13 August 2022

70377700R10024